America's Game
Kansas City Royals

Paul Joseph

ABDO & Daughters
PUBLISHING

Mitchellville
Elementary Library

Published by Abdo & Daughters, 4940 Viking Dr., Suite 622, Edina, MN 55435.

Copyright ©1997 by Abdo Consulting Group, Inc., Pentagon Tower, P.O. Box 36036, Minneapolis, Minnesota 55435. International copyrights reserved in all countries. No part of this book may be reproduced in any form without written permission from the publisher. Printed in the United States.

Cover photo: Allsport, pages 5, 27.
Interior photos: Wide World Photo, pages 1, 8, 10, 13, 14, 15, 17, 20, 22, 25, 26

Edited by Kal Gronvall

Library of Congress Cataloging–in–Publication Data

Joseph, Paul, 1970-
   Kansas City Royals / Paul Joseph
      p. cm. — (America's game)
   Includes index.
   Summary: The history of the Kansas City Royals, an expansion team that took the field in 1969.
   ISBN   1-56239-667-6
   1. Kansas City Royals (Baseball team)—Juvenile literature.
[1. Kansas City Royals (Baseball team) 2. Baseball—History.]
I. Title. II. Series.
GV875.K3J67 1997
796.357'64'0978139—dc20   96-16086
                                              CIP
                                               AC

Contents

Kansas City Royals 4

The Royals Are Born 7

"Sweet Lou" 8

Continuing To Build 9

If You Build It, They Will Come 10

The Royals' Legend 12

Supporting Cast 14

One Step Away 16

Darn Yankees 17

Not Again! 20

Finally! 21

The 1980 World Series 23

Surprise Finish 24

The I-70 Series 25

Highs And Lows 26

The Legend Retires 27

A Great Franchise 28

Glossary 29

Index 31

Kansas City Royals

The Kansas City Royals have brought a lot of excitement to Missouri baseball fans and to the entire Midwest. As an expansion franchise that took the field in 1969, the Royals have accomplished a lot in their short history.

The Royals have captured the American League (AL) West Division six times, two American League Championships, and took the greatest baseball prize of all by becoming the 1985 World Series Champions.

Within their first 10 years, the Royals were considered a mini-dynasty, and they challenged the best teams in baseball for the championship. By the Royals' 11th year, they were already in a World Series.

The Kansas City Royals have never finished a season in last place. That is a remarkable feat for any team, especially for an expansion team.

The Royals did well because owner Ewing Kauffman recruited the best baseball people to be part of the Royals' staff. He built his

Facing page: Royals' slugger George Brett smacks another homer.

organization from the ground up. First he got top-notch front office people. Then he hired excellent coaches and scouts, who in turn found great players.

Pitching was the key to the Royals' success, along with outstanding hitters. One of those hitters was Hall-of-Famer George Brett. Brett was a pure hitter who played the game with every ounce of energy he had.

Since the Royals' introduction to the professional world, they have won many games and attracted many loyal fans. The Royals always seem to be at the top in attendance. But if it weren't for a team that left Kansas City for Oakland, the Royals may have never been established, let alone become the great organization they are today.

The Royals Are Born

Professional baseball first came to Kansas City in 1955 with the arrival of the Athletics, formerly of Philadelphia. Even though they never had a winning season, there was great fan support for the Athletics in Kansas City.

In 1967, the team had promising new talent with the likes of Reggie Jackson and Jim "Catfish" Hunter. But owner Charlie O. Finley, who was looking for more money and a better deal, moved the team to Oakland.

Kansas City fans were shocked and angry. Ewing M. Kauffman, a wealthy Kansas City businessman, believed it would be best for the community to quickly get another baseball franchise. It didn't take long to get a new team. Since the city had supported baseball so well, they were awarded a team within months of losing the Athletics.

Kauffman became the owner of the team and named them the Kansas City Royals. The new uniforms were white and royal blue, and they had a simple KC logo on their hats. The Royals were in the American League West Division, and began play in 1969.

Lou Piniella slides safely back to first base.

"Sweet Lou"

Fielding a brand new team is one of the most difficult jobs in all of pro sports. Kauffman admitted that he knew very little about the sport into which he had just invested millions. So he simply went out and hired the best baseball people to run the front office.

First he signed a general manager, Cedric Tallis. Tallis came to Kansas City from the California Angels. He was an aggressive executive who told the Kansas City fans that they would have a World Series Championship team in a very short time.

Tallis then signed the best scouts to help him find the talent to make a real winner. First of all, he hired Joe Gordon as manager. Now it was time to build the team with players. The Royals got players from the expansion draft, the regular draft, and from trades.

The best known of the first-year Royals was outfielder Lou Piniella. "Sweet Lou" played baseball with all his heart, every day. He would go on to play 17 years in the majors and continue coaching after that. Piniella had the honor of having the first base hit for the Royals on Opening Day, April 8, 1969. The Royals went on to win their historic first game against the Minnesota Twins.

The Royals finished their first season with a 69-93 record for a fourth-place finish in the American League West. Piniella hit .282, with 11 home runs, and 68 RBIs. He was also name Rookie of the Year.

Continuing To Build

With lots of money, good trades, and wise draft picks, the Kansas City Royals continued to improve. By the end of the 1970 season, the lineup included outfielder Amos Otis, shortstop Fred Patek, second baseman Cookie Rojas, and catcher Jerry May. A new manager also joined the team—Bob Lemon.

Lemon was an old-style baseball man. Under him the Royals had their first winning season in 1971. Their 85-76 record was good for second place in the division.

Unfortunately, 1972 was different. The team finished with a 76-78 record. Kauffman became disappointed with the staff. First he fired Tallis, and at the end of the season he fired Bob Lemon. Kauffman decided to hire a young manager to run the show. That man was Jack McKeon.

In his first year, McKeon turned the team around with an 88-73 record and a second-place finish. But in 1974, the Royals dropped to fifth place, winning only 77 games. The players didn't like McKeon very well. So Kauffman, also taking McKeon's poor record into account, fired him in July 1975.

Although the early 1970s were up and down for the Royals, they did have some exciting things happen that would forever be a part of the Royals' tradition. One was a Royal Palace and the other was the start of a legend.

If You Build It, They Will Come

Because of their poor record and many personnel problems, the Royals finished 1972 in disarray. But on opening night in 1973, a jam-packed, standing-room-only crowd endured the bitter cold and snow to see the brand-new Royals Stadium.

Royals Stadium in Kansas City, Missouri.

Royals Stadium was a state-of-the-art ballpark built only for baseball. It replaced Kansas City's Municipal Stadium as the team's new home. The new stadium was a beautiful facility, with fountains of water in the middle of a pool behind the center field fence.

Royals Stadium was the first park in the American League to feature artificial turf in the infield and outfield. This new turf helped the Royals. Opponents had a hard time judging ground balls because of the strange hops they took.

Once the Royals were used to playing in this stadium they took full advantage of it. The Royals found that by hitting slicing line drives to the corners they would turn into inside-the-park home runs, and hard shots over the shortstop might go all the way to the wall for extra bases.

Someone who took full advantage of this new stadium was a young California native named George Brett, who was just beginning his incredible career.

The Royals' Legend

In 1973, the Royals not only got a new stadium but they also got a player who would become the heart and soul of the Royals for the next 20 years.

George Brett led the Royals to a World Series Championship, two American League Championships, and six AL West Titles. The future Hall-of-Famer would go on to capture three batting titles and the AL Most Valuable Player (MVP) Award.

It all began for Brett and the Royals in 1973, when he played 13 games after the regular third basemen, Paul Schaal, got hurt. Although Brett did not play that well, the team knew that he was their future third baseman. In 1974, the Royals traded Schaal, making George Brett the new third baseman.

Brett was hitting only .200 at the 1974 All-Star break. Not happy with his offensive performance, he used that All-Star break to work with hitting coach Charley Lau. From then on, Brett took batting practice from Lau before every game. It became a regular routine for both of them.

Brett became a hitting sensation, giving most of the credit to Lau. Brett went on to win his first of three batting titles in 1976. His best hitting year was in 1980, when he flirted with .400 the entire season. He finished the year batting .390 and added another batting title to his list of honors.

George Brett watches his 3,000th hit sail away in a game against the California Angels, September 30, 1992.

In his 17th season (1990) he won his third batting title! Brett, who has said he'd like to be remembered "as a guy who always played hard and ran out every ball," is the only player in the history of baseball to win the batting title in three different decades.

Second baseman Frank White fires to first base to complete a double play.

Supporting Cast

Everyone knew that Brett was the best Kansas City player, but he could not win the games alone. Luckily, the Royals had a good supporting cast and considerable talent by the mid-1970s.

Along with Brett, outfielder Amos Otis, designated hitter Hal McRae, first baseman John Mayberry, and second baseman Frank White formed a very strong offensive attack.

Pitchers Steve Busby, Dennis Leonard, Paul Splittorff, and Larry Gura held other teams to little or no runs. With this potent nucleus, the Royals were becoming a mini-dynasty and were contending for the World Series.

Amos Otis belts another hit in a 1982 game against the California Angels.

Whitey Herzog was named manager of the Royals in the middle of the 1975 season. For Herzog, the major hurdle for the Royals was their arch rival, the Oakland Athletics, the former Kansas City team. The A's had won the AL West the last four years in a row, and it looked as if 1975 would be a repeat performance.

Surprisingly, in 1976 the Royals won the AL West, but not without a struggle with the A's throughout the season.

After the Royals clinched the AL West, two Kansas City players—Cookie Rojas and Freddie Patek—braved the cold October chill and took a victory swim in the fountains at Royals Stadium.

Royals' fans and all of the players were very excited that the team had finally made it into the playoffs. George Brett later said, "Nothing will ever be as sweet as our first division pennant in '76, because we'd never been there before. The first one is extra special."

Royals' right hander Dennis Leonard fires a pitch during a 1977 game against the New York Yankees.

One Step Away

Although winning their first pennant was very special, trying to get past the next point was very difficult. In their first playoff series in 1976, the Royals faced the AL East champion New York Yankees.

In a seesaw series, the Yankees captured the first game, 4-1, after the Royals lost their star outfielder, Amos Otis, to a broken ankle. Kansas City came back to win the second game, 7-3. The Yankees took the third game, 5-3.

The fourth game was a do-or-die contest for the Royals. If they won, they would force a fifth and final game. If they lost, the season would be over. Trailing most of the game, the Royals made a remarkable comeback and stole the game, 7-4.

The final game was exciting. Each team wanted desperately to make it to the World Series. In the eighth inning, with the Royals down by three runs, and all of the New York fans at Yankee Stadium believing that their team was headed to the World Series, George Brett stepped up to the plate. With two men on base, Brett hit a towering home run to tie the game! The Royals thought they might win the game.

But the Yankees had other plans. They were not about to give up. In the bottom of the ninth inning New York's Chris Chambliss hit a solo home run to win the American League title. The Yankees were on their way to the World Series.

John Mayberry is tagged out at third base during Game 3 of the ALCS against the New York Yankees.

Darn Yankees

In 1977, the Royals earned a franchise-record 102 victories and their second AL West title in a row. Those 102 victories included one stretch of winning 16 in a row and 24 out of 25. To this day, Whitey Herzog believes that the 1977 Royals were the best team that he had ever coached, and George Brett says that it is the best team he ever played on. But to get to the World Series that year they would have to get by the Yankees again.

In the best-of-five American League Championship Series (ALCS), the Royals jumped out to a 2-1 series lead. In the fourth game, the Yankees pulled off a 6-4 victory, sending the series to a fifth game.

The Royals led the game 3-2 going into the ninth inning. Kansas City was very confident because the game was on their own turf. If they held the Yankees scoreless, they would go to the World Series.

But it was not to be. In the top of the ninth inning, the Royals made some critical errors and pitched poorly. The Yankees did some clutch hitting and scored three runs. In the bottom of the ninth, the Royals couldn't muster anything. The Yankees again were headed to the World Series, and the best team in Royals history had to watch it on TV.

Kansas City

Lou Piniella made the first hit for the Royals on Opening Day, April 8, 1969.

Hall-of-Famer George Brett joined the Royals in 1973. During his career he captured three batting titles.

Second baseman Frank White helped form a potent offense for the Royals in the mid-1970s.

Outfielder Amos Otis joined the Royals' lineup during the 1970 season.

Royals

In the mid-1970s, pitcher Dennis Leonard helped the Royals become World Series contenders.

Willie Aikens hit a single that scored the winning run during Game 3 of the 1980 World Series.

Bret Saberhagen was a star during the Royals' pennant-winning 1985 season.

Outfielder Bo Jackson was the first Royal to hit 25 home runs and steal 25 bases in one season.

Not Again!

The Royals won their third straight AL West title in 1978 with 92 victories. Again they ran into their nemesis—the New York Yankees. They split the first two games, with the Yankees crushing the Royals 7-1 in Game 1 behind the powerful hitting of Reggie Jackson. The Royals bounced back to win Game 2 in a tight back-and-forth 10-9 contest.

The third game was very close, and could have gone either way. George Brett hit three home runs, but it wasn't enough as the Yankees pulled off a 6-5 win. The Royals could not rebound after that and lost the fourth game and another ALCS to the Yankees, who headed to their third-straight World Series.

Everyone involved with the Royals' organization—from the owner, to the front office, to the coaches and players, and especially the fans—were heartbroken. Three great teams and no World Series.

Everyone was down, and it showed in the 1979 season as the Royals couldn't recapture the AL West title. Whitey Herzog was fired and Jim Frey took over as manager for the start of the 1980 season.

Pete LaCock evades Yankee shortstop Bucky Dent to steal second base during Game 1 of the 1978 ALCS.

Finally!

The Royals got back on track in 1980 in a big way. They finished the season with 97 wins and their fourth AL West Title in five years. They also moved themselves into the national spotlight as one of the most dominant teams in the American League. Leading the way was the legend himself, George Brett.

Although Brett played with nagging injuries the entire season, he kept his batting average above .400 for half the season. No one had hit above .400 since Ted Williams in 1941.

Brett finished the season batting an incredible .390, the closest anyone has come to .400 in the American League since Williams. It earned Brett his second batting title.

More important, Brett led his team into the playoffs and another shot at the World Series. Guess who the Royals had to beat to make it to the World Series? You guessed it, the New York Yankees!

Everyone involved with the Royals couldn't forget losing three in a row to the Yankees. But the Royals grabbed two quick wins on their home turf, with a crushing 7-2 Game 1 victory and a tight 3-2 Game 2 win.

The Royals were not overconfident about winning two games. They were off to New York to win the American League crown.

In the seventh inning of Game 3, with two outs, the Yankees had a close 2-1 lead. With two men on, George Brett came to the plate. Brett sent the very first pitch over the right field wall, all the way to the third deck of the seats, for a three-run homer and a 4-2 lead they would never give up.

Two innings later it was all over. Finally, after so many years of trying and coming up short to the Yankees, the Royals had won the American League Pennant and were heading to their first-ever World Series.

Willie Aikens lashes a single to left-center field to score the winning run in Game 3 of the 1980 World Series against the Philadelphia Phillies.

The 1980 World Series

On Tuesday, October 14, 1980, the Royals played their first World Series game against the National League Champion Philadelphia Phillies. Game 1 was played in Philadelphia, and the Royals jumped out to an early 4-0 lead. The lead didn't last long, however. In the third, fourth, and fifth innings, the Phillies scored seven unanswered runs. The Royals rallied in the ninth, only to come up short, 7-6.

Game 2 was another heartbreaker for the Royals, who grabbed an early lead only to lose it late in the game. The Phillies won Game 2, coming from behind 6-4.

Game 3 was historic for the Royals organization. They won their first-ever World Series game in exciting fashion. The Series had now moved to Kansas City, and the score was tied 3-3 after nine innings. In the bottom of the tenth, with two men on first and second, the Royals' Willie Mays Aikens hit a single that scored the winning run.

In Game 4, Aikens was the hero again with two home runs as the Royals won 5-3 to tie the World Series at 2-2.

Game 5 would be the last game in Kansas City, and the Royals were confident they could head to Philadelphia with a 3-2 lead. And it looked like that was going to happen as they held the lead in the ninth inning. But, for the third time in the Series, the Phillies came from behind to win 4-3.

The Series returned to Philadelphia, and the Phillies had control the entire game, winning 4-1 and capturing the World Series. But the fans of Kansas City were still proud of their Royals!

Surprise Finish

After their World Series appearance, the Royals were predicted to do well. But a strike-shortened season, injuries, and drug problems with key players left the team in disarray.

Before the 1984 season, the experts picked the Royals to finish last. But the Royals didn't listen to the experts, winning 44 of their last 69 games to capture a surprising AL West title.

Although they were swept 3-0 in the ALCS by the Detroit Tigers, they had a lot to look forward to. "In a way, we should be embarrassed by our performance in the playoffs, but the way our young pitchers pitched, we've got a lot to look forward to," said George Brett.

And Brett was right. Young pitchers Bret Saberhagen, Mark Gubicza, and Danny Jackson turned into stars during the 1985 season, leading the Royals to their second-straight AL West title.

In the ALCS against the Toronto Blue Jays, it looked like the Royals were going to be swept again. The Royals were down 2-0 in the series, which was now expanded to seven games. And with the score 5-2 in the third game, it looked all but over. Then George Brett came alive—hitting two home runs, a double, and a single to lift the Royals to a 6-5 victory.

The Jays won Game 4, taking a 3-1 series lead. It was the last win for the Jays. The Royals won three in a row to steal the American League Pennant. They were on their way to their second World Series.

The Kansas City Royals celebrate their 1985 World Series triumph over the St. Louis Cardinals.

The I-70 Series

The 1985 World Series was a matchup between Missouri's professional baseball franchises—the Royals and the St. Louis Cardinals. People called it the "I-70 Series," referring to the interstate highway that links the two cities.

After two games in Kansas City, the Royals were down 2-0. They headed to St. Louis for the next three games, and many felt that the Series would never return to Kansas City. If the Cards didn't sweep the Series, they would surely end it in St. Louis.

The Royals got a "must win" in Game 3, winning 6-1. The Cardinals won Game 4 and were one game from a World Series title. But the Royals won two in a row and tied the Series at three games each.

The seventh and final game was played at Kansas City. After losing two in a row, St. Louis couldn't rebound, and the Royals crushed them 11-0. The Royals were World Series Champions for the first time in franchise history!

Highs And Lows

After the Royals' 1985 World Series title, the team began to play poorly. Injuries, managerial changes, free agency, and retirement led to their demise. Their best showing was in 1989, when they finished second with a 92-70 record.

In 1986 the Royals signed a superstar who didn't help them win, but drew huge crowds to watch him play.

Vincent Edward Jackson—better known as Bo—was the best college football player in the nation, but he decided to play baseball instead. In his first at-bat as a Royal he hit a thunderous home run. The following year he decided to play both baseball *and* professional football, joining the Los Angeles Raiders as a running back!

Jackson was the first Royal to hit 25 home runs and steal 25 bases in 1 season. He was also named the All-Star Game's Most Valuable Player in 1989. Meanwhile, as a running back for the Raiders, he averaged 5.5 yards per carry and was selected to the Pro Bowl.

In 1991, a serious hip injury ended Jackson's baseball and football careers.

Outfielder Bo Jackson follows through on a swing during a 1987 game against the Seattle Mariners.

The Legend Retires

George Brett continued to hit as the Royals struggled. In 1990 Brett earned his historic third batting title in his third decade. In 1992 Brett smacked his 3,000th career base hit, a milestone shared by only a handful of the greatest players.

As the Royals played better baseball, trying to capture the AL West Title in 1993, Brett thought about retirement. The Royals finished with a respectable 84-78 record, good for third place in the division. Brett finished the year and an incredible 20-year career with a single up the middle for his 3,154th—and last—hit.

George Brett is honored after smacking his 3,000th career hit, September 30, 1992.

A Great Franchise

Although the Kansas City Royals are a relatively young franchise, they have done some great things. At one point they were considered a mini-dynasty, winning 6 AL West Titles in a 10-year span. During that time, they made it to the World Series twice and were World Champions once.

The fans continue to be the backbone of this great franchise. The Royals have averaged 2.2 million in attendance every year since 1980, being the envy of most clubs in Major League Baseball.

Putting a winner on the field will be the only way to continue their successful tradition. In 1994, Major League Baseball realigned the divisions, adding a Central Division to each league. The season, though, was awash when the players went on strike.

In 1995, the Royals began their climb towards the top as they finished in second place. It was the start of the comeback trail that could lead to another World Championship.

Glossary

All-Star: A player who is voted by fans as the best player at one position in a given year.

American League (AL): An association of baseball teams formed in 1900 which make up one-half of the major leagues.

American League Championship Series (ALCS): A best-of-seven-game playoff with the winner going to the World Series to face the National League Champions.

Batting Average: A baseball statistic calculated by dividing a batter's hits by the number of times at bat.

Earned Run Average (ERA): A baseball statistic which calculates the average number of runs a pitcher gives up per nine innings of work.

Fielding Average: A baseball statistic which calculates a fielder's success rate based on the number of chances the player has to record an out.

Hall of Fame: A memorial for the greatest baseball players of all time located in Cooperstown, New York.

Home Run (HR): A play in baseball where a batter hits the ball over the outfield fence scoring everyone on base as well as the batter.

Major Leagues: The highest ranking associations of professional baseball teams in the world, currently consisting of the American and National Baseball Leagues.

Minor Leagues: A system of professional baseball leagues at levels below Major League Baseball.

National League (NL): An association of baseball teams formed in 1876 which make up one-half of the major leagues.

National League Championship Series (NLCS): A best-of-seven-game playoff with the winner going to the World Series to face the American League Champions.

Pennant: A flag which symbolizes the championship of a professional baseball league.

Pitcher: The player on a baseball team who throws the ball for the batter to hit. The pitcher stands on a mound and pitches the ball toward the strike zone area above the plate.

Plate: The place on a baseball field where a player stands to bat. It is used to determine the width of the strike zone. Forming the point of the diamond-shaped field, it is the final goal a base runner must reach to score a run.

RBI: A baseball statistic standing for *runs batted in*. Players receive an RBI for each run that scores on their hits.

Rookie: A first-year player, especially in a professional sport.

Slugging Percentage: A statistic which points out a player's ability to hit for extra bases by taking the number of total bases hit and dividing it by the number of at bats.

Stolen Base: A play in baseball when a base runner advances to the next base while the pitcher is delivering his pitch.

Strikeout: A play in baseball when a batter is called out for failing to put the ball in play after the pitcher has delivered three strikes.

Triple Crown: A rare accomplishment when a single player finishes a season leading their league in batting average, home runs, and RBIs. A pitcher can win a Triple Crown by leading the league in wins, ERA, and strikeouts.

Walk: A play in baseball when a batter receives four pitches out of the strike zone and is allowed to go to first base.

World Series: The championship of Major League Baseball played since 1903 between the pennant winners from the American and National Leagues.

Index

A
Aikens, Willie Mays   23
All-Star Game   26
American League (AL)   4, 7, 8, 11, 12, 15, 16, 17, 20, 21, 22, 24, 27, 28
American League Championship Series (ALCS)   17, 20, 24
American League Central Division   28
American League East Division   16
American League West Division   4, 7
artificial turf   11

B
Brett, George   6, 11, 12, 13, 14, 15, 16, 17, 20, 21, 24, 27
Busby, Steve   14

C
Chambliss, Chris   16

D
Detroit Tigers   24

F
Finley, Charlie O.   7
Frey, Jim   20

G
Gordon, Joe   8
Gubicza, Mark   24
Gura, Larry   14

H
Herzog, Whitey   15, 17, 20
Hunter, Jim "Catfish"   7

J
Jackson, Danny   24
Jackson, Reggie   7, 20
Jackson, Vincent Edward (Bo)   26

K
Kauffman, Ewing M.   4, 7, 8, 9

L
Lau, Charley   12
Lemon, Bob   9
Leonard, Dennis   14
Los Angeles Raiders   26

M
May, Jerry   9
Mayberry, John   14
McKeon, Jack   9
McRae, Hal   14
Most Valuable Player (MVP)   12
Municipal Stadium   11

N
New York Yankees   16, 17, 20, 21, 22

O
Oakland Athletics   15
Otis, Amos   9, 14, 16

P
Patek, Fred   9, 15
Philadelphia Athletics   7
Philadelphia Phillies   23
Piniella, Lou   8
Pro Bowl   26

R
Rojas, Cookie   9, 15
Rookie of the Year   8
Royals Stadium   10, 11, 15

S
Saberhagen, Bret   24
Schaal, Paul   12
Splittorff, Paul   14
St. Louis Cardinals   25

T
Tallis, Cedric   8, 9
Toronto Blue Jays   24

W
White, Frank   14
Williams, Ted   21
World Series   4, 8, 12, 14, 16, 17, 20, 21, 22, 23, 24, 25, 26, 28